The Pain That Produced the Oil

By Carmen Barnes

Copyright © 2018 by Carmen Barnes

All rights reserved. Published by Carmen Barnes no part of this book may be reproduced or transmitted in any form or by any means, electronic or mechanical, including photocopying, recording, or by any information storage and retrieval system, without written permission from the publisher.

ISBN 978-1-725-08000-3

This book contains certain events that have taken place in my life. It describes part of the past painful experiences as well as obstacles that I've overcome. Prayerfully, this will encourage and give you the strength to overcome your past.

THE PAIN THAT PRODUCED THE OIL

Introduction

This book was written to help others become victorious in their journey to do what God has called and anointed them to do. Sometimes people experience unusual battles and life relationships that seem to have no purpose. After multiple such encounters, I realized the purpose during each stage was to destroy what was hidden deep inside me. It was to keep me from reaching the spiritual level of maturity to reach the lost and release the oil of prophecy for God's people. "Thou preparest a table before me in the presence of mine enemies: thou anointest my head with oil; my cup runneth over." *Psalm 23:5 (KJV)*

I was three-years-old when I had my first demonic encounter. I recalled seeing dark spirits roaming around the house. These spirits would be on the wall lurking and looking. At first I could only see them, but then I started to hear movements, sounds and chattering, but I told no one. Back then, it wasn't unusual for me to look into a dark room and see several sets of eyes staring back at me. One day, one of these spirits stood behind me and I screamed loudly. When my mother heard the screech and came into the room, she saw the fearful expression on my face, and she knew what I had seen. She knew that stricken look because she had been able to see spirits since she was a child. My Grandmother came into the room and with a knowing heart, she prayed over me. At this age, I was very sensitive, spiritually. After that experience, my grandmother kept me close.

My father is adopted and my mother is of Haitian decent. My mother is Christian. Although English is my first language and I was born in the United States, I speak Creole, understand French and speak Twi (pronounced twee) a dialect of the Akan language spoken in southern and central Ghana. My Grandmother and Great grandmother on my mother's side were Haitians, and they were spirit-filled believers who were Church of God in Christ and Pentecostal. We lived on the east coast in Pennsylvania – a deeply religious and very spiritual family.

Teaching about spirits and the supernatural were limited when I was growing up. What I learned, I picked up from listening to our church leaders and reading materials. The late Dr. Miles Monroe was one of the teachers I listened to. The more I listened, the more I put things together in my own mind. My Grandmother told me to "Call on the name of Jesus" and to "Plead the blood" when I saw these spirits.

Much later, I discovered that I had a prophetic anointing that allowed me to be able to see into the spirit realm, but I didn't know that these spirits would attack me and try to attach themselves to me through relationships. Their goal was to utterly destroy me spiritually, emotionally, mentally, and physically. Thank God – no weapon that is formed against me shall prosper!

Although I went through storms and fires, bitter relationships and abuse, I persevered. Yes, I have scars and disappointments, but they did not penetrate my heart or my love and commitment to God. Yes, I waivered and faltered, but I did not stop getting back up and I still have the anointing oil of God. I'm here! I'm free! And, I'm happier, stronger and more focused than I've ever been – committed to doing the work of the Lord!

"But the anointing that you received from him abides in you, and you have no need that anyone should teach you. But as his anointing teaches you about everything, and is true, and is no lie – just as it has taught you, abide in him." I John 2:27

Chapter 1

In January, as my sixth birthday drew near, it was also around the same time my biological father took my little brothers and me to McDonald's to get something to eat as he promised. I remember that day well because when we left McDonald's, he bought me a yellow scooter.

A few days later, my mother had another man in the house; all I could remember was her telling the other man, "Here he comes!" The man ran into the closet and stood there. When my father came home, he began to question my mother as if something was wrong. My father kept eye contact with me as I cued him towards the closet. After a few minutes had gone by from them arguing back and forth, my father decided to open the closet door, and there he found the other man inside.

That was the day all hell broke loose in the house. My grandmother had to come and get us because she didn't want me to see what was happening. My mother was so blind mentally, it was ridiculous.

I remember my mother was so angry with me that day that she slapped. She slapped me so hard that I fell into the water heater. She said I remind her of my father. (Anyone who grew up on the East Coast in Philadelphia, New Jersey, or New York, could tell you that those water heaters were dangerously hot!)

That was also the last time I saw my biological father as a child. Once he left, my mother told me I had ruined her life. As a young child, those words stuck with me and followed me, even into my adulthood. *That was an attack on my emotions.*

•

After a year passed, my mother married the same man my father found in the closet. Often, I wondered, "How could she be so selfish?" I felt that she chose that relationship for no reason at all. What did she see in him? Just by observing him, I felt that he was no good. He would always watch my every move to see what I would do. As every child should be, I was protective of my mother, so every move she made I was right there watching him. I felt like I had to be her eyes because she wasn't as attentive as she should have been. I didn't feel as though she would make good decisions because of her actions. As time went on, her new husband became abusive.

One night, I woke up out the middle of my sleep to find my Great Grandmother sitting downstairs. As I walked down the stairs, I saw trails of blood. I asked my Great Gram where my mother was, and all she said was she'd be back. Deep inside, I instantly knew something was wrong! Every morning I would watch Benny Hinn "This is your day." Benny Hinn said, "Touch the screen," and on the day she came home, I did as I would every morning.

When I heard the door open, I noticed my Grandmother was slowly escorting my mother into the house. As my mother entered, I was surprised to see that she had a neck brace on, her eyes were nearly swollen shut, one arm was in a sling and she was walking on crutches. I soon found out she had broken ribs and a broken jaw! I immediately became angry! From the moment I saw my mother's physical appearance, I knew that man was responsible for this and I hated him for it!

As my mother sat there on the couch, she could barely see me for the swelling, but she just stared at me. Even at that age, I remember touching her body and singing, "I am The Lord that healed thee." and as I sang, I cried. Immediately my mother's eyes opened and she could move her arm. She grabbed me and cried. At that moment, my grandmother and great-grandmother knew what I carried spiritually. From that point on, they taught me how to pray and nurtured me. *That was my spiritual awakening. I had a gift of discernment and a gift of healing*

My Grandmother was a member of a Pentecostal Church and she would take me to early Morning Prayer two or three times a week. I heard my Grandmother pray specific prayers for people. I learned to bind and loose and to rebuke the devil. I learned that you pray and take authority over the enemy for your family. I learned to pray, but I still needed to know God for myself.

While my mother recovered, that evil husband of hers never came to the house, that's how I knew he was at fault. I couldn't wait to get my hands on that evil man. Although I was quiet, once I became angry, I knew I could hurt someone. That day finally came.

One afternoon, my two little brothers and I were outside playing, and my mother's husband appeared. Before he got to the door, my brothers, and I attacked him with empty bottles and glass, we found on the ground and we continued beating him until we saw blood. That's when I knew we had gotten him good, and the neighbors on the street had to rush over to take us off him. After that, it appeared that things got worse. My mother began using drugs, and I would find men coming back and forth and finding colorful condoms on the closet shelf. I used to get so tired because while my mother was away for hours at a time, they left me at eight and nine year's old, babysitting four siblings.

I was angry about being left to raise my brothers and sisters and to raise myself. I didn't know it then, but without proper guidance, I was susceptible to the people around me and not all of them had good intentions.

One afternoon, I went home and there was no one there. So, a neighbor who was older than me invited me over to her house; this young lady's mother allowed anything in her home. While upstairs playing and watching television, the young lady said let's play house, so I said okay. She told me to take off my clothes, so I did. She began to get too close to the point it became uncomfortable. I remember she touched me and made me touch her; she even made me kiss her. I knew something was wrong when she told me not to tell anyone about what had taken place. When I returned home, I began to stare out the window as if I was waiting on something amazing to happen.

This was the first physical attack on my body, my character and my emotions. An unwanted sexual advance allowed a spirit of perversion to attach to me. Because I didn't know what this was, I didn't know how to pray about it and I was too ashamed to talk about it. That was just what the enemy wanted. He wanted to put me in a place of secrets.

These events took place during the time my mother was out in the streets or when she allowed those men from the streets to enter our home. My Grandmother was so tired of what was happening. It had gotten to the point that I would fall asleep at school because I stayed up all night babysitting. The school threatened to take me away from my mother, and that is when my Grandmother intervened. During this time, she enrolled me into a Christian school. I didn't like it because my siblings weren't getting the same treatment. I felt changing schools wouldn't make a difference because I would still have to go home to the same situation.

As a child, I tried to give my siblings anything that I had because I didn't want them to grow up thinking I was better than they were. There were times I would even save my little coins from picking up lint particles off the carpet floor of my Grandmother's house. As the oldest child, it was my responsibility to care for the younger ones. The money I earned cleaning was the same money I used at the corner store to buy bread, milk and eggs to cook for them. As the big sister, I was also their protector.

As my Grandmother took us away, my mother pleaded and begged my Grandmother to let us stay, but it was far too late. Although I was unhappy, I was also very excited. Who wouldn't want to be in a better environment? While at my Grandmother's house, my siblings and I bathed and ate well. On top all of that, we had a lot more television stations and it was exciting! As weeks passed, my mother decided she was well enough to take us back. In my mind, I didn't want to leave because my siblings were happy and eating well. Who would want to return to unpleasant conditions? But, I didn't want to see my mother upset, so we decided to go back with her.

One thing about my mother back then, she had a tendency of doing well for a few weeks and then allowing her habits and addictions to overtake her. I knew she was a good person, but as long as other things including different men, influenced her, her mind would be partially on us. When we arrived home it started off well, but then my mother was hurtful towards me.

My mother had no problem leaving alone at a young age, and that led to unwelcome attention and further abuse. When I was eleven years old, I remember being home alone and the housing authority maintenance men would randomly show up to our house. One day after I had showered, one of the men came into my room while I was naked. What happened next left me feeling dirty and ashamed. Since that day, I was never the same again. It felt as though in that moment, the world stopped and paused for me. It was as if I was the only person on earth. I thought to myself, "How could something like this happen? What did I do wrong?" I questioned myself and began blaming myself for what happened. Unusual thoughts began overtaking my mind, and I knew that the spirit of perversion was lingering on me.

Another secret has been created, another strike to my emotions and another demonic attack has succeeded. Perverse spirits will attack anywhere there is an open door. Unfortunately, I did not know how to protect myself, and I felt my mother didn't care. This too was a trick and attack of the enemy to make me think I wasn't love and what happened to me didn't matter.

As time passed, my mother met this new man at the church we attended, and he began to come around more. At this point, I was 12-years-old. I couldn't stand to see another man coming around again. They dated for two years, and then came another sibling. My attitude began to change. At first, I was angry because that meant another child for me to babysit. I thought to myself, "This can't be life! How on earth can you have more children and we are already lacking?"

Often, I viewed my mother as selfish because her needs always became before us. Here we are with pretty much nothing yet another man and another baby. When my little sister arrived, I was happy because that made three girls. What angered me the most was never being able to touch or play with her? I knew this wasn't good, so I disliked this new man too. Inside, I thought he felt his child was better than me. Six months after my youngest sister arrived, my mother married him. The man she married was okay, but then things changed.

He moved us out of the projects and we lived in a real house in a much better place. At least I was happy about that. A few months later, here comes yet another sibling and that made five boys. We moved into a real nice place.

Chapter 2

I was always told that I was acted older beyond my years. As I grew older, I grew wiser, but I was still naïve about the world and the things in it. I developed few friendships as a teenager and poured myself into academics and sports, ignoring the spiritual awakening inside me and accepting the pull of the sin nature.

Because I was different, what worked for my siblings didn't necessarily work for me. Running track most of my teen age life always kept my head clear. Whenever I was angry, I would just go outside and race the cars in the neighborhood. As time went on, changes happened, and my mind began to wonder.

I was always a private person growing up. I attended church and played sports. That's all I knew. Sports at the time were my life. It always gave me something to look forward to when I had nothing else. I always stayed in a world of my own and was always told that I was different compared to everyone else. People would tell me that I had an old soul in a young person's body because I was well above my age mentally, spiritually, physically and emotionally. I never expressed my emotions openly. Even grown men would think I was older because of my conversation and maturity level.

When I was 14-years-old in the ninth grade, I ran track and played basketball. I was an exceptional athlete and student while attending high school. Going to school where no one knew me was difficult. I was very intelligent and had excellent grades; that was the year I won the National English Merit Award and Who's Who among Americas' Top Students. Although I was popular in sports and academics, I lacked in the social areas of my life. I never knew how to communicate effectively. Even though I knew what I wanted to say, I never knew how to verbalize it openly.

There were times I would walk the halls during class change and girls would look at me funny, laugh at me, and call me names. I never understood why I didn't have friends or why no one really cared to be my friend. No matter how much I tried to fit in, it never worked. To see other guys and girls in relationships or hugged up around the lockers and eating lunch together in the cafeteria bothered me. I would often ask myself, "What is it that I don't have? Or what am I doing wrong?" Knowing that most of the girls were not as beautiful or attractive as I was, and that they didn't have long hair as I did, confused me.

Here I was thinking more outer appearance because my body was more in shape from being in sports. Though I knew there was more than what it appeared to be, I could not recognize it at that moment. The ninth grade was tough because I realized more about myself and knew nothing about boys or relationships. However, there was this one young man who was sweet and befriended me.

This young man would follow me everywhere, wait until I finished track practice and even walk me home from the track field. My siblings loved him. He would come to the house just to play video games with them. He was silent and stayed to himself. He was my only friend. In my last year of high school, he moved to Maryland, and I never saw him again. That was the worst feeling ever.

•

While on the track team, I had a guy teammate who lived close and we hung out. We would walk from practice together and to the bus stop together. Every morning I would go to his house to meet him so I wasn't alone. My teammate was a cool guy, and my parents liked him. My Grandmother taught him in school. My Grandmother was a teacher at the school, so she knew everyone in the building - teachers and students.

My track teammate asked me to attend the 12th grade prom with him in 1999 because he and his girlfriend broke up. I asked my Mother and Stepfather, and they told me no. I said, huh? This makes little sense! Isn't this what seniors look forward to? I shouted, "You already know him!" For the past four years he's been coming over sitting, eating and hanging out. So once again, they said no! I couldn't believe my ears I yelled, "This is just stupid!" So, that was one major life event I missed out on apart from me qualifying for the Olympics because my parents said I was too young to travel to Atlanta with the school's coach.

At that point I became rebellious. I started sneaking out of my window at night to hang out with different boy. I wanted to prove myself and I did the unthinkable. This young man's father was well known in the city and had businesses across town. His father was also the deacon at his church. This young man was very sneaky and on the football and baseball team. Often, he would act as if he were so innocent and did no wrong.

Night after night, I sneaked out and he would come pick me up in his white car. We would go to his house late at night as if we were studying and just hang out. Knowing it was wrong, I didn't care. We would sneak to his father's store and do things we had no business doing. I was in so deep I couldn't get out! I had a reverence for God, but I was so deep in sin I wore it like a coat. Not only that, but I believed it was okay because everyone, including church members, were doing it.

•

Summer break was always exciting to me! Every summer I took part in FCA camp (Fellowship of Christian Athletes) where I was a camp counselor and huddle leader. I looked forward to this every year. I would meet new people from all over the country and it was cool! I was a track coach, and I enjoyed every minute. At 16, I was preparing myself for college. I had to because my parents pulled me out of school.

Because I had excellent grades and high test scores, the school officials wanted me to skip a grade, but my parents objected. Then they did the unthinkable. They pulled me out of school and made me take the GED exam. I passed at 16, so my next step was to go to college.

Until then, at least I was going to summer camp. However, my last camp visit wasn't my best one.

That year during a camp, I met a man about 24 years older than I was. This man had intentions that I was not aware of. (I didn't know at the time that he was married and had children older than me.) He was active in church preaching and coaching basketball. I remember we had fun times. I fell asleep in his roommate's room after we went out to eat. He never bothered waking me, but instead left me in the bed asleep. What happened next made what was innocent on my part, seem wrong. The director came into the room and saw me sleeping and he became crazy. After that, the coach could no longer come back to camp, and I was too ashamed to speak although nothing happened.

The coach was a postal worker and would call me in between his breaks. It got to where he would stop and see me. But here's the thing - he was married. He took me seriously, and I had no clue thinking it was friendly. After a while, he would write me notes and say little things and offer to take me places and I refused. I became concerned and asked my mother about fornication and she suspected something.

One day my mother heard me on the phone chatting with this guy and somehow, she got a hold of his number and called him to meet. That's when his wife found out about me. Because of my demeanor and conversation she had no clue. I was only 16-years-old. During the conversation while his wife and father-in-law who was the pastor of their church was present, he stated that he was in love with me. I felt so bad because I was in the middle of an affair I knew nothing about or how it happened.

This last camp visit helped me realize what a soul tie was and that it had to be broken. I had a gift of teaching and was wise, but I was also very gullible. Unbeknownst to me, these actions caused my character to be attacked and began to hinder my growth from the inevitable.

It took a while to get over this situation because he continued to contact me. However, out of first wisdom and then respect for his wife and family, I blocked his contacts, changed my social media contacts and forbade him to make contact with me again.

•

During the same week, we had a visiting group come to the church I had known since I was 14, and in this group was the one guy I would become interested in. When he and his group arrived to the church, some grown women were jealous of me because he only wanted to talk with me. The group invited me and two others from church that were like cousins to travel with them to another church function. One woman from the church found out about my friendship with the guy, and told the Pastor, and they said none of us could go. After that the group never wanted to come back there. Never understood what was wrong with me. I was just lost. I had to get away! Fortunately for me, I already had plans to leave.

After I passed my GED, I had a choice of colleges and scholarship offers to attend college on the west coast or the east coast. I chose the east coast. So Florida here I come!

While I was in college in Miami the church group guy and I kept in touch, and he even came down to Miami to visit while he was at a concert. We spoke so much to where I fell in love with this man, talking to him daily. This was a serious soul tie. He was the one talking about marriage. But he ended up ministering in California. I was transferring to UCLA to be closer to him. Maybe a year after we were talking he called in disappointment one evening and said a woman from a church he attended brought him a bottle of water and the next thing he knows they had sex and she was pregnant! It crushed me! I said what is going on with me? Either the man sleeps around on me or he's married. I didn't have sex with any of them. It hurt me so bad, and it took me a long time to get over this guy, but eventually I did.

Chapter 3

The transition to Miami was smooth and fun. Little did I know that wicked spirits were waiting to dupe and lull me into a place of complacency all in the name of love. A spirit of manipulation to control my physical and my spiritual life began through the man who would be my husband. First, he introduced me to his church. While it seemed harmless at first, eventually, this spirit grew in strength and confidence, leaving me in a state of mental and physical confusion.

In November 2000, I was attending a university in Miami. While in the student recreation hall playing pool and watching television, this guy walked through with a suitcase, and he looked just like the guy from the group and I stared then looked away. He looked as if he wanted to speak, but he didn't so I left and went to my dorm. The next day I went to class and saw the same guy passing by and he looked. I smiled and kept walking.

Later that evening I went down to the recreation center for a smoothie before going to play basketball and once again I saw this man. I headed to the door and he stopped me and asked me my name. When I told him my name, he laughed, and said it must be a coincidence because we have similar names. He invited me to church, and I said of what time Sunday should I be ready? He said it's Saturday at 10 a.m. and I said okay.

Now, it's Saturday and I am preparing to attend service. He came to my room to escort me to the car, and so we are having small talk about where we are both from. I knew he was from another country as well, and when he said Haiti I smiled, and told him that's where my grandfather was from. Then we pulled up to the church and we went inside. As soon as I went in, he introduced me to some friends, and immediately I noticed it was different. It was a Seventh Day Adventist Church - something I wasn't used to.

After service I sat and watched him sing with his band, and I thought here we go again a singer. After rehearsing with his group, on the way back to the dorm, we stopped at a Haitian restaurant and the dish was one of my favorites, Legume. While eating, we chatted about sports and other things. Then I went home and studied.

Later that evening after showering, I heard a knock at my door and it was the young man. I asked him what he was doing here, and he said he wanted to see me. I said okay and we went to the lounge on my floor to sit and watch television. That night he stayed with me, and we fell asleep watching a movie and it was cool.

When we woke up, I told him to go home and rest. Later that evening I went out to get fresh air on the roof. I went up and played basketball, I and after about an hour this same young man came to the rooftop and challenged me in a game. That was one of the most exciting times I had in school.

After the game he asked me what he had to do to be Mr. Right! I said for him to be himself, that's all. The following day, I went to his house and met his mother. She was very nice and greeted me in French and brought me grapes. While at his house, I noticed that we had some of the same books, so we studied together.

That was the first night I slept at his house. I kind of wish I hadn't. That's the night he lost his virginity. I said how on earth is this happening? He was a sweetheart, and he was 26-years-old. I thought "What does this man see in me?" After that we were always together, and I moved in with him, which was a horrible mistake.

He worked security overnight on Miami Beach, so I would go to work with him to keep him company. Whenever he was hungry, I would walk to 7-Eleven to grab him some food. The view on the beach was beautiful, and I would just sit and think of my life and what I wanted to accomplish. All I wanted was to be happy and at that moment I was. I did whatever I could to please him. As time went on, it was like I became someone I'm not. I attended church with him regularly, and when I wanted to find another church to attend on Sunday, he would make it difficult for me.

Every evening we would play ball at Cagney Park in North Miami Beach and play ball at Pepper Park on 135th Street on Sunday Evening. I then met old high school buddies of his and began getting more comfortable with his family. Life was simple for me. I continued my studies and my course work did not suffer.

Later that year, he joined the Navy and the same week he joined, he left. Before he left, he suggested that I visit home which was Pennsylvania since I didn't have family in Miami. He bought me a one-way ticket, and I cried the whole way home.

Once I stopped crying and thought about it, I decided to take the test to join the Navy and I passed with flying colors. Yes, I was in the process of joining the Navy. My high score allowed me to choose any field I wanted, so I chose the medical field. I was going to be a heart surgeon. The Navy gave me time to make sure this is what I wanted to do before they shipped me out. I was 18-years-old, and I was able to get extensions until I made a final decision about the Navy.

During my time in Pennsylvania, I spent days with my Aunt, Grandmother and Great Grandmother. Even though he was away, he called daily. As weeks went by, suddenly the calls stopped.

One day I went for a ride to Delaware. While in Delaware, I met a handsome guy from Kenya. I heard him speaking, so I asked, "What part are you from - Uganda or Kenya?" He replied, "Kenya." Afterward, we exchanged phone numbers because he had to continue his day.

After leaving the restaurant later that evening, he asked me if I wanted to meet up, and I said I didn't mind but, I had just met him. He came to the house where I was and met my family. They loved him and he seemed like a sweetheart, so I sat and watched him interact with everyone. This young man smiled, and I was a little uncomfortable, but he was African and that's my culture, so I didn't feel so bad. Later that week, we went to a park for a walk and played soccer because that was the only sport he could play. Although he loved watching American football, soccer was his thing.

After we left the park, we went to eat, and he invited me over. I sat on the sofa and relaxed. While watching the game he went to the fridge to grab a beer. He would drink and drink until he passed out. That evening he fell asleep halfway on the floor so I took him to his room, and I straightened up the area where we sat. I ended up spending the night. I decided since I had a new friend that maybe I should plan to stay in Delaware. It worked out well because the base wasn't that far from where I was.

I got a civilian job overnight working in a nursing home. It sucked so because he and I both worked overnight. Since he and I were always together, he asked me to move in, so I did. That's the night things changed again.

One evening after taking a bath, I noticed female items that were still in his closet on the shelf. So, I asked him what was up with those items? His response was, "Oh that's my ex's!" I let it go after that. Day by day as time went on, I noticed he would work later and later. Sometimes he worked doubles and I became worried.

On a morning I just so happen to be home, there was a knock on the door. It was his ex-girlfriend. She was a thin blonde-haired woman with glasses staring back at me. As I opened the door, I kindly asked her, "How may I help you?" She asked if he was home and I said no.

My stomach was so hot! I couldn't believe she had the nerve to show up and then try to leave a message. I was angry. So, when he came home I asked him who she was and why did she come, and he said, "Oh, probably looking for me." I had nothing to say. The thoughts in my head began to move a million miles per minute. My instincts told me that he was still seeing her, but he thought I was crying for other reasons.

After a few days had gone by, he decided to leave for two days. Within those two days, I had a friend over. Although I knew it was wrong, I didn't care. Nothing happened, but it was the fact I had this guy over. We spoke and caught up on old-times from camp years earlier, and I said you know what I need to rest we will keep in touch!

When morning came, I was cleaning and took out the garbage. On my way to the garbage I saw our neighbor's brother. Though he spoke, he kept watching me. I went inside and days later this same guy appeared and kept asking me questions. I told him I was seeing someone. He said, "Oh yea, he got a girl already." I was shocked. When he then asked me if I worked at night? I thought, "Hmm, maybe she comes over during the time I am at work." I then ended our conversation. I was to the point that where nothing that happened would make me cry anymore just because I've been hurt so many times dealing with these men.

After a year of being together, I packed up my belongings and left. When I was getting ready to leave my phone rang. Guess who it was - my ex-boyfriend from Miami?! Years had gone by, and my ex from Miami found me after all that while saying he was on the ship for six months and then they sent him for another tour. I heard his laugh, and I knew it was him, and I asked how did you find me? He said, "Duh I work for the government of course I'll find you."

He told me they stationed him in Norfolk. Surprisingly, he asked me to come visit him, so instead of going to Pennsylvania, I went to visit him in Virginia. When I arrived I had no clue where he was or if he had changed. To my surprise, he had changed. He seemed like he was better, happier and was trying to do better with his life.

We spent time together and caught up on things. He heard I was seeing someone, and I mentioned how he neglected me. He told me he called daily but my grandmother refused to tell. At the end of my visit we agreed to keep in touch. As I headed back to Pennsylvania I thought, what's going on with me? What have I become?

Chapter 4

Although I knew The Lord, sang and prayed, I had no real relationship with Him. All the while I had a void that only he could fill. I would cry out to God and then go right back to what I wanted to do. I felt like I was too far away to come back to him. I even quit going to all of those churches there. I had a little reverence for God, but not a total commitment. I knew of him, but I wasn't walking with him. My anointing was so diminished and dark at that time. God was still moving and functioning in my life, but it wasn't at a higher level. He was so merciful to me. It was a place of acknowledgement where I knew God was holy and I had to have a change in my life.

I had relatives and cousins there in Pennsylvania that couldn't stand me. They never really got to know me and didn't want too because I differed from them and their mothers were closer to their parents than mine. They always frowned upon my siblings and me because we didn't have things like they did. Mind you those were my mother's sisters. They always thought they were better.

I ended up going to Philly to visit friends, and we went to this African night club. I danced my hips off that night! While there I met this guy from Nigeria. We kind of hit it off and kept in touch. Eventually, I visited his house. It was just a place to chill out and relax. Before I knew it, I was called over all the time because he wanted to see me. I did not care; I didn't even want a relationship anymore. I said at least I wouldn't get too attached to him. We visited off and on for months at a time. Even while I was out-of-state we kept in touch.

During this course of time while talking with my friend from Nigeria, I met a guy from Sierra Leone. We became friendly and hung out daily; I even went over his house where he and his roommate stayed along with his roommate's girlfriend. They were cool people, and I enjoyed their company.

After months of seeing each other, I noticed unusual behaviors. I thought he was homosexual, but I still didn't stop seeing him. I would drive around in his fancy red Lexus and got whatever I wanted. This man did anything for me. We met up with church friends and just had a great time dancing and laughing. They would even come over to the house to eat and chill. Although I had reverence for God my flesh overcame me.

I was so far away it was scary. I was sleeping with this man not caring or anything. I already felt like it was over so I didn't even bother to attend Medical School as I should have. I had planned to become a nursing practitioner, but that fell by the wayside when I lost my focus. We threw parties and drank so much. *Even in all of this, I still knew who the Lord was. I would hear his voice speaking and giving me direction. It confused me and I still refused to listen.*

I moved back to my grandmother's house and during this time my great-gram stayed with her. Every day I asked if my ex-boyfriend from Miami called. While sitting on the sofa reading a book one day, he called. (I didn't realize I was so in love with this man that dropped me as if I had no existence.) I answered the phone call, and I was already an emotional wreck because of my emotions and men. (I just kept attracting weird guys, but it was like something always drew them to me. That was a familiar spirit.)

So I went to meet him at the naval base in Virginia, and when I arrived my brother was there and said he found my real father. I went to see if it was true but I never met up with my father? My brother said he had his own place there and I found out it wasn't true. There were four other people there - a girl with her three kids and her cousin. The house had so much traffic all the time people coming and going. I thought what's going on here? Either this is a whore house or a drug house. I was so uncomfortable.

My ex-boyfriend from Miami called, and I told him I had to leave immediately because I didn't know what was going on. That night I stayed in the barracks and got rest. I was tired of the turn my life was taking.

•

He and I started where we left off a few years earlier. It was a Friday morning, and he came to pick me up. He said to get dressed and let's go out. That day I thought nothing of it, so I dressed simply and we ended up at a building with a county clerk to get married. That was Friday the 13 of June, the same day I got orders to Parris Island in South Carolina.

I was happy that I got married and did something right. We both got sent to South Carolina and moved into base housing. Things were going okay for the first few months then I found out he couldn't keep his money. I thought what's going on? He was sending every dime he had to his mother in Miami. His mother worked, but she sent everything to Haiti. He was so attached to her he would go broke.

When his mother found out we were married, at first she was nice, but then she flipped the switch on me. She hated my guts. When I asked him, he said it was none of my business. That was the beginning of a life altering experience. As time passed, we would do things like play basketball and watch a movie here and there. Then came text messages and late-night phone calls.

I would hear the phone ring at 11p.m. and 1 a.m. I would ask who was calling this time of night and his response was, "A friend." That was the same night he locked me out of our bedroom and refused to let me in. He told me if I knocked or banged on the door again he would get me. I had no choice but to go in the other bedroom and sit on the cold floor with no blankets or anything. We didn't have furniture in the house so it was bad for me. He refused to even get furniture because all the money would go to his family and friends. Mind you, we stayed on base housing, so we had Basic Housing Allowance.

There was no way for our money to keep running short with both of our paychecks. I had to end up getting a second job where I worked in town at Burke's Outlet. It was as if he didn't care at all because he demanded all money go to him. That was the night I left the house and walked to the MP's office. I didn't have a choice, and they put him in a barracks for a few days. He had anger issues that were crazy. They had to separate us to keep us from fighting. I could not have friends or talk to anyone; he took my cell phone and mailed it to his mother in Miami.

Here I was with nothing and no one. One day that next week on lunch, I went to the gym to play ball and one of my buddies noticed something different about me. He said you don't look well at all. Usually you can jump for a rebound with no problem, but today you barely got off the ground. As I continued to play, I began sweating like crazy and nearly passed out. Someone sent me to the Naval Hospital that afternoon. When I arrived to the hospital they ran a lot of tests.

The hospital checked me out and said I could go home to rest. About an hour after I left, the hospital nurse called me with news. She said I was pregnant. I was thinking it's been nearly two years since we married, and I'm just now getting pregnant. I thought it was a sign, and I ignored it. I remember calling my mother immediately telling my family the news, and all I heard was screaming. My siblings were excited screaming "Carm's having a baby." I was excited, scared and every other emotion, all at the same time.

When my husband arrived home, I told him the news, and all he said was, "Wow!" I thought things would get better in all of this, but it didn't. I worked so much during the pregnancy I got pre-eclampsia, toxemia and gestational diabetes. I wasn't able to rest because I worked two jobs and did his homework studies for him too!

I was lost and didn't know who I was anymore. I was living for him instead of myself. Every dime went to him. I only went clothes shopping once and could only get a few clearance items but nothing I wanted.

My doctors hospitalized me because of excessive swelling. I was so sick. My skin darkened, and I couldn't hold anything down. All I wanted to do was sleep, but fortunately, my husband told me not to sleep and rushed me to the ER. I constantly had to have my urine checked for proteins and other medical conditions. My blood pressure was steadily rising and my blood was toxic. To my dismay and excitement, my Mother walked into my room. She said she had passed by my room several times because she did not recognize me I was so swollen and disfigured. My mother had found out about my condition from relatives and what was happening, and she came there to take care of me.

A few days later, here comes the joy of my life, my son. He was so handsome, and I couldn't believe I was really a mother. But, I was so ill I could barely hold him and nearly dropped him because I would just fall asleep from the medications. Even my biological father came to see about me after my son was born.

The day we left the hospital, my mother went home first to prepare the house for us. This was the first time I had seen my mother in years. I couldn't believe she came all the way to South Carolina to help me, especially since I had been away since I was 16 to attend college out-of-state.

Immediately after I got home, this man (my husband) laid down on the futon and told me to make him some noodles. Keep in mind, I had just left the hospital a few minutes ago, and I was told to rest because I had a C-section and couldn't lift or do much. My mother was upstairs and heard what he said. She came down and said, "If I hear you doing anything when I leave, you are leaving." My mother made phone calls and left to get back home.

However, my husband never changed. He started to help a little and then he quit. I called my mother and told her, and then my biological father came and drove me and my son to Pennsylvania.

Chapter 5

Going back to Pennsylvania was so hard because I was embarrassed. I was the only one out of my cousins and a few aunts to be married before having a child. I know that may be good; however, the circumstances were painful.

My husband was in South Carolina and I wasn't there. I stayed for about three weeks and it got to the point where people tried to run my life telling me what I should and shouldn't do. I was tired of all the opinions because my mother spoke too much and my family knew too much about my personal life.

Out of shame, I left with my son and flew to North Carolina where my biological father wanted to meet with me. When I arrived, it was okay at first, but then he spoke nonsense, so we left again and went back. He started trying to tell me what I need to do and how I needed to live. He wanted me to divorce my husband. (He really couldn't stand him.) In my mind I would have been a failure, and I didn't want to hear what anyone had to say, even though it was true.

Although he wasn't perfect, he was still my husband, so I decided to deal with it the best I could. I went back to him in South Carolina. I was so angry with my life at this point. We moved to Camp Lejeune, North Carolina, and I felt comfortable with a few people I met. They were cool to be with. We had been in North Carolina for about two years, and as we prepared for the big move to Miami, I became tense. I remembered how his mother couldn't stand me.

When we arrived, she took my son and didn't acknowledge me. While we stayed there, I did all I could to help and worked in Cutler Ridge, in south Miami, Florida.

We had two vehicles, and the one I drove, he decided to donate for tax money. I would apply for jobs for him away in Atlanta and Naples, Florida. He needed to get a better job, and I wanted to get away from his mother. I had to do everything for him – even help him look for and apply for jobs. I told him that I didn't want to be in the house with that woman. I was the only one working, and it was stressful after a while.

I had to put my plans on hold daily to suit his needs. I became pregnant with my daughter during this time, and decided to find a good church and started attending.

I was active in praise and worship and traveling with my friend to various churches to sing, which I enjoyed every bit. Only one person was unhappy that I was going back to church, and that was my husband. In order to please him, I attended the Seventh Day Adventist Church he took me too a few years back while in college. I did whatever it took to make him happy and to keep the arguing minimal. They baptized me in the Seventh Day Adventist Church, and that really angered me because all I wanted to do was make him happy.

While there, I met the girls that were calling my house in South Carolina at 1 a.m. (The first think I thought was that they could have at least been cute!) Anyway, my husband knew I was angry and tried to start an argument so he could blame me. Also, about this time, I found out that he was talking to another woman over the phone again and she wasn't in town either.

Now, here I am with a newborn baby girl that I had just given birth to. I was hospitalized longer than usual because of high stress levels. While in the hospital, the doctors told me that they gave me a tubal ligation after delivery. I was so drugged due to the amount of medication they gave me that I couldn't think.

This man told the doctors to sterilize me, so I couldn't have any more children! He made me sign the permission papers, and I had no clue what they were for. Even in the hospital, he carried an orange folder threatening to divorce me if I didn't follow his rules. Because of the pull he had, he could get away with anything. I was so medicated that I wasn't aware of anything at all.

After being released a few days later, I still could not use the bathroom. I was very unhappy when I had to leave my two children with their father and his mother because I was going through hell with them both. I also found out he was giving all the doctors and nurses hell, so they took it out on me. I had a catheter that gave me an infection, and I could not use the bathroom.

I remember calling my great-grandmother because I knew she had a direct line to heaven. As I told her what was happening, she told me to place my hand over my belly. As she prayed immediately, it was like my water broke and I was able to use the bathroom. When I got home after the last doctor's visit, I prayed and sought-after God. I knew I needed help because I couldn't do it on my own and it was bad.

•

I saw how his mother wanted me dead and was practicing voodoo on me. I saw it and new about it. I was starting to become more in tune with the Godly spiritual realm then. I saw the candles in the house and my husband actually told me and admitted that he used to go to Ft. Lauderdale to meet with a witch doctor to try to have things done to me, but it didn't work. His mother would try to physically attack me because she was frustrated with the "black magic" not working. He wouldn't divorce me because I benefited him.

It was hard because I was in that house and strongholds were everywhere. I knew how to pray even then and she hated it. I would be in my room listening to worship music, and she would bang the door cursing me out in Creole. I never said a word to her. My husband heard her and knew she did it, but he refused to tell her to quit.

Every day I would see things and feel spirits in the house. Because it wasn't my domain, I could only pray. She loved darkness in the house, and she could never be in the same room with me. The house always smelled foul, and it would literally make me sick. Imagine the stench of a sewer mixed with the sickening sweet smell of incense.

Every three days I was hospitalized with anxiety and given prescriptions as if I was crazy. This lasted a whole year. It made me angry because she (his mother) would treat me badly but then ask for my help. I taught her English and took her shopping all the time. She went to Haiti and came back with scabies, and I still helped her because that was the right thing to do. Even through this she still wanted me dead. She told me I'm no good, go back where I came from and leave her son. I'm not good for him. She had so much control over him and he was so blind to it.

One night I heard him on the phone speaking like he was hiding and I knew he was talking to another woman. I got to the point where there was no need for me to even question him. He was a control freak. I was already angry because his mother would go behind after I cooked and make him another meal as if she were competing with me. I was sick of her ways. That same week, I ended up in the hospital again with another anxiety attack. Whenever I was away, his mother was more excited. I could sense it and feel it.

The person I saw in the mirror I no longer recognized. I was numb of all feeling and just wanted out. I honestly was tired of praying for a man who refused to change. He told me point blank this is how I am and that is it. I asked him constantly "Do you love me"? His response was "Actions speak louder than words."

His response really became clear that the actions he showed me were not that of one in love. He more so tolerated me and what I could do for him. He always said how intelligent I was and that no matter what a person did, I would always forgive. I realized that I was just foolish. I asked myself what have I become? All of this nonsense is making me sick. I needed a change and no one could help me - not even family. For him, everything was just about money.

•

I blamed myself daily for what I was going through. He would constantly curse me and call me names. He would humiliate me in front of his friends and belittle me in front of his mother. This is when I was hospitalized every two weeks with anxiety and panic attacks. I knew in my heart something had to change; I just didn't know what or how to do so. I would think if only there were a way out I'd take it. I attended service that evening, and I always made sure I took care of home first before leaving.

After coming from church in West Palm Beach that night, I realized I no longer had a key to the house, and he and his mother had locked the doors. I came through the side door and knocked for 20 minutes while he sat there watching me as he looked at the game on television. I had my children with me and my daughter was only a few months old. I was so cold. My church musician took me to his house so the children could sleep. All I remember is crying for days at a time. Here I am with two children and nowhere to go.

In the spring, I ended up staying at the musician's house for a few weeks because my then husband refused to let us come home. He constantly ridiculed me for no reason because he was unhappy with his life. He wanted me miserable because he was.

While staying at the musician's house, he fell for me and I was not interested. He knew my situation and wanted to help, however, his mind was elsewhere. I got tired of people taking advantage of my situation and I felt obligated because they were helping me. Eventually, my friend's mother questioned his getting involved with me, given what was going with my life. We stopped seeing each other.

•

Overall, I was just tired, and things became too much. I never really understood what was wrong with me or why I seemed to attract weird men. I know they saw the anointing on my life and that's part of what attracted them to me.

On a deeper note, it wasn't just the anointing. There was a garment covering me. The garment of lust, perversion, control and manipulation was on me. These things all resulted from the experiences I had as a young child and a young woman. There were strongholds that needed to be broken off of my life. Every time I decided to do right, I would fall into temptation again.

Here I am separated from my husband when I met a popular man in the SDA church. He was sweet and helpful, but I wondered what else did he want? This man would allow me to come by his house and he would stay from time to time at my house. I disliked the fact he could only be seen with me certain places and at church. But, at other programs he'd ignore me until the services ended. I was good enough for everything that had to do with in-house but not out in public. I found out this man had asthma and I would be there monitoring him and giving him medicines and teas. (I've always been a good care giver to anyone I know.)

There were many times a certain woman would always appear at the house while I was there or he took her places alone. One day I questioned him and we got into a huge physical altercation in his room. I left his house and walked to find a bus to get home.

One Saturday I found out that this popular man was at someone's house and I always wondered why he was there. The one woman I suspected had hooked him up with her sister. She knew about me, but felt her sister was better. The outcome was that he was weak and ended up with the sister. She got pregnant then they married. Then he had the nerve and audacity to locate me after all he's done saying asking if he could still see me from time to time.

During this time of separation, my divorce was finalized. By then, we had both been honorably discharged from the Navy. My ex-husband kept the children because I didn't have a place to stay. Mind you, I didn't have a car because he got everything in the divorce. In the meantime, I had to find a house for us.

This was a trying time because my ex-husband had custody of our children and refused to allow me to see my kids. All 13 years down the drain. I often pondered on the times my ex-husband would kick me out of our room to sleep on the floor in another room just so he could talk to his so-called friend. (What married man answers a call at 1 a.m. to speak to a "friend?")

Soon, I found out that all along he (my ex-husband) was talking with a young girl in her twenties, sending her "our" money in the Dominican Republic, and he went there many times to see her. I met her while going past the house to see my kids. I hated leaving them, hearing their cries. It was so hurtful to know he told my daughter's teacher I left them.

On Mother's Day they asked all the children to make something for their mothers and the teacher found my daughter sitting with her head down. The teacher asked her what was wrong, and she responded, "I don't know where my mommy is." It devastated me to find out he told them I left and moved to North Carolina which was untrue. I used to sit outside their father's house every night just to make sure they were safe until the lights went out. It was a very hurtful experiencing.

After being homeless for so long, in October 2010, I received a call from the housing authority saying the place I applied to was available and to come get the keys. I remember rushing so fast to get there. I got the keys, went upstairs praying and dropped to the floor thanking God! I had a place for my kids and me to live together again. My son was five-years-old and a baby girl was two-years-old. Once the kid's father found out I had my place, he tried to come over. He would come because he wanted to have sex with me as if I was his prostitute. Whenever I rejected he'd get angry. There were times I knew that I needed the money or things for the kids and he'd bribe me to get what he wanted. Afterwards, I'd feel so dirty all I could do was cry, and I remember him giving me that orange envelope with divorce papers and DNA tests for our children.

It hurt to know this same man I gave my young adult life to would pretty much treat me like I'm nothing or as if I slept around - and that's not how I was at all. The DNA tests for both children came back at 99.999% his children. Still, at the time, I felt like a failure.

I was attending church singing on the Praise Team and praying, and all yet, I was still living in sin. I felt so out-of-place until I heard the pastor say I needed to leave and find somewhere to go because I'd never let people get too close.

Chapter 6

My mother found my number and called me to say I needed to leave Miami and come to Arkansas. She said if I didn't leave something would happen. So now fear had come in. I purchased plane tickets for my kids and me to leave immediately. When we arrived, my mother and stepfather picked us up and took us to their home. Though it wasn't enough space, we stayed for three months. I knew it was time to go. They said they were moving and had a place for us to stay.

The children and I ended up staying in a house with people who abused drugs and alcohol. They gave me and my kids a space in a garage where there were dog feces and flies. I couldn't sleep. I would go days not sleeping just to watch the kids sleep comfortably. I managed to get phone service since there was no reception for cell phones in that area.

This was shelter living. I was the only black person there which made it uncomfortable. I would clean my area and the house. I was praying and trying to do right. There was something that those people I was in the shelter with saw in me and that was the Holy Spirit. They always told me their issues and that they needed prayer. The prayer would work and they would move out and get their own places. I became so frustrated not being able to have food because my mother wouldn't let us stay with her.

I didn't want to, but I called my ex-husband and told him I needed to leave, and he said to come back home. He bought us tickets and we flew back home to Miami.

When we arrived, we stayed with a friend until I had a plan. I met up with an old friend and stayed at his place for a few days. I didn't like his lifestyle, but I had to suck it up to have a place to rest. One day, his best friend came over and we chatted and got close. He was a sweet man but he was going through a divorce. Such an amazing guy! We got so close that he would take me to his mom's house, and we'd stay the night. As weeks went by, we moved in together - such a bad Idea. Later, I found that his mother was practicing voodoo too.

(Same smells. Same anger. Candles burning.) She wanted me to marry her son. She demanded I demanded I marry her son, but we were just friends. We were not in a relationship. I soon left, but it wasn't long before another relationship would begin.

•

The spirit of manipulation knows no boundaries, has no shame and is capable of traveling through social media. (At this time, I was not discerning anything because I was totally out of the will of God, so it was impossible for me to hear His warning.) I was searching for something and didn't know it.

Out the blue – I received a contact from a Pastor in Ghana – on Facebook. He was staying in Nigeria, but he was from Ghana. I was already planning on visiting Ghana to visit my big brother since there was nothing else for me to do. This Pastor was living in Nigeria but was Ghanaian. We chatted daily for weeks and the crazy thing is there were red flags that I chose to ignore.

Months later, I purchased my ticket and while there visiting, I stayed close to him for a month. We ended up getting married and I came back pregnant. That's the crazy part. My tubes were tied. This man wanted a child badly, and prayed that I would get pregnant.

Imagine my surprise when I found out he believed in voodoo too. This was a long distance relationship, because I traveled back and forth. He was supposed to come to the States, but he couldn't get a passport.

I found out the hard way that my Ghanian husband was living a double life. He would always hide his cell phone or receive calls late in the evening. I was so tired I was ready to go. When I arrived back to Miami while exercising I cramped and miscarried. This man had me so blind to the point I'd give everything I had to make sure he was okay. The spirit of deceit and manipulation was so strong on him I would believe anything he said, even if I knew it was a lie. I knew it was more to him than he told me. I did everything within my power to bring him here. It would never work. They denied him a visa three times. He became so angry with me to the point of disrespect and having his pastors call me. I never met his mother while I was there, and I knew it was serious.

The following morning, I received a message from a woman claiming to be his fiancé. She pretty much recalled every conversation that he and I had down from the beginning and I couldn't believe my ears. She even mentioned the rings I had for us because he gave them to her. This man denied everything and said he was being blackmailed and watched. He was actually nervous because he couldn't believe the truth was coming out.

His true side really came out when I stopped sending him money. I found out he was in the middle of building a church with the money I sent. That was his way of trying to keep me close to him, so he could complete his evil project.

•

During this time I was living in Miami when I met an Apostle from the Bahamas. I was his assistant and would drive to Orlando weekly and stayed at his home to assist him in service by praying and leading worship. We would go everywhere together in my car. Apostle was extremely jealous that I was married to the Ghanian. The crazy thing is he was married to someone, but they were separated and never divorced. I would never question it because it wasn't any of my concern. I got to the point where I was tired of doing so much for this person and not seeing the fruit of his labor. I always felt that if God "chose" him for that he would provide and provision was already made.

As time passed, I saw no changes in the Apostle and his behavior and his mouth was vulgar. I knew once and for all this had to end so I ignored his calls and not responding to him. I know now I should have spoken to him but at the time he would not have been receptive because of his state of mind. "Apostle" would disrespect me calling me a whore and a slut. He would curse me and call me a "nobody." I couldn't believe a so-called man of God would treat me in such a way after assisting him as I did.

I realized there was a cycle, and I had to get out! There was a pattern of a pastor or a "Man of God" trying to locate me or converse with me to drain my oil. They knew what I carried, but I was yet to find out myself. I knew I needed to break free, but I didn't know how or who to trust.

●

Prayer changes things! One evening I arrived at my friend's house and prayed to God. I said God if it's meant for me to leave Miami please make a way for my kids. After praying I looked at the windows and eyes literally watched me. As I walked inside, I could feel being watched. Immediately I prayed and covered myself. The next morning I woke up and was pressed in my spirit to pick up my babies. Right before then, I received a call that some money was being sent to me and I cried. I first called Greyhound to find the next bus leaving for Arkansas, and it was leaving out in three hours. I was trying to find a way to get the kids and go. A few minutes later my good friend's brother showed up and said he'd take us so off we went to get the kids and went to Greyhound in Miami Gardens.

As I purchased the tickets, no one knew of our leaving we just had to leave everything behind. Once we left Florida, the entire ride all I could do was thank God although I was uncertain how things would turn out. My children and I arrived back to Arkansas and this time I came with more power and anointing than the first time. *Now I knew what to watch for and what to stay away from. I also knew how to pray for myself and my children.*

I was staying my family in Cabot and the Lord dealt with me on so many levels. I would stay in my area fast and pray for days at a time just to hear what the Lord was saying or trying to show me. I landed a great job for the State and working in mental health. I could save and get a vehicle to attend church and work. I was only receiving between 100 and 200 dollars every two weeks from the children's father to make sure they were taken care of. I started my side hustle baking cupcakes and making money from that.

I always felt as if my mother was competing with me in everything I did, and I would always hear her voice in the back of my head saying, "I won't let you or anyone else ruin my marriage." It would bother me because it would take me back to how she interfered with my marriage calling him and telling him all kinds of things that would make him not trust me.

One day, my sister and I were getting picked up from work because my van got repossessed. I couldn't make payments and give my family money too. While headed home, I noticed my stepfather was texting my mother telling them he was on the way. As we pulled up inside the house, I saw the electricity off and my children and nephew sitting holding flashlights. I was furious! I went to the bathroom to give him the money I took from the ATM to add to my share of stay at their house. Immediately my stepfather jumped in my face and disrespected me and my mother allowed it. Every week I was using all my money to pay for pre-payed electric to the point I was broke.

There was so much going on in this house to where I couldn't agree. My siblings were living all kinds of lives as they pleased, and yet they were preaching the gospel to other people. I couldn't stand it! I asked my mother why she would let that man disrespect my children and me, and she said she heard nothing. I cried for days. It always seemed when something was wrong then, they would need my help or need me for prayer. I was good enough to pray because they always saw results, yet they would treat me badly.

At this time, I was in consecration with a dry fast. It went to the room and cried out to the Lord. I laid down on the floor and felt like I was dozing off. All of a sudden, I heard harps and streams. I turned my head to open my eyes to see and my room was fogged up. My Mom could not enter my room because of the cloud in my room. All hell broke loose.

One evening my stepfather gave me an ultimatum and put my children and me out. I was relieved because I didn't have to deal with anyone anymore nor the bedbugs. Two young ladies from church were always so helpful. One of them came all the way to Cabot to pick up my kids and me to take us to the shelter.

Here is where ministry took place for me. Immediately as I arrived I was embarrassed. I couldn't believe it had come to this again. I instantly thought back to the kids being taken away from me by their father because I had no place to live. I used to have to take baths at McDonald's or a friend's home. I then realized this was an internal issue.

My mind needed renewing because I couldn't think well. As they gave me my bed space a woman looked at me and said, "Why are you here? You don't belong here." When the evening came, the women asked me to pray with them and I couldn't understand anything that was happening. As I prayed, the presence of God fell so heavy these women cried and fell to their knees. The office workers came out and seemed like everyone in the building stopped for prayer. Afterwards, I went to the bathroom and prayed and cried. I asked to Lord to help me and show me what to do. I said, "Lord you brought me here, now show me what to do." At this moment, I realized it was never about me. I stayed for one month and I got a job working at Target and a local bank. God sent help. I really felt that things were getting better for me.

Chapter 7

One Tuesday evening, a church member took us to church. My then Apostle called me up to the front and told everyone I needed a place to stay because I was homeless. I had no clue what was happening. I was on the Praise Team and Prayer Team, so for people to hear this made many saw me in a different light because I was so private. This same evening a fellow church member took me aside and assisted me.

My church member picked up me and children and she took me to fill out my application for Section 8. She actually helped me get my first place and until this day I am forever grateful. (That same evening, I had a dream that my family lost their home and I saw the man, the date it happened and when he told them.) I could take part in a Re-home Program because it determined me to get out of the shelter. It was like The Lord had everything being lined up for me. Someone gave me a voucher where they paid my rent for three months. All I could do was shout and praise God!

With Christmas nearing, I was concerned about my children getting things they needed. Our House shelter and Re-home brought my children uniforms, school supplies, toys, bikes clothes and shoes. They even gave me a Wal-Mart gift card to purchase my uniforms, hygiene products and shoes for work. I saw how blessed I was even in that situation.

On Christmas, my family came from Cabot to visit us in our home and then my little brother made it a habit to spend the night. I knew something was going on. Suddenly I had to move my things to another place because I lost that one. It seemed odd.

I was working every day and one day I asked my mom to keep an eye out on the kids since there was no school and it was snowing. That's when they told me they were homeless and had no place to stay. I let them keep the left side of my place which had the rooms and a full bathroom. Keep in mind the way they treated me because I never disrespected them or looked down on them. I had to forgive. I allowed them to stay. As time passed, they ended up moving into their own place.

•

It was a Thursday evening and I was working my shift at Target as a supervisor. There was this guy who would come and sit inside Starbucks at 5:15 p.m. daily. It was like he was watching me or something. I heard someone say "Etesian" and I looked around because I knew the language was Ghanaian Twi. I turned and responded and when I did, he said that's all he knew. He stated his name and I greeted him. He began to ask a lot of questions, so I invited him to attend church with me that Sunday.

The next Sunday morning, I picked him up, and we went to church. On the way there, the previous man I dated called arguing, and that was when it was over for us. My new friend heard this, and it's like he ran with it. He and I chatted and during this time I was transitioning yet again into another apartment.

This man helped me move everything into my storage unit. The children and I stayed with my brother in Cabot for a few days. One day as I was leaving work, I sat outside after dropping him off. He noticed that I was still outside his apartment complex, so he knew something was wrong. It was 1 a.m. and my babies were asleep in the car. This man invited us up, but I was hesitant. He knew I would not compromise like I would have done earlier and he promised to leave his space to us. This young man was away a lot, so it was like we had the place to ourselves. Here this is a 58-year-old man in this situation.

As time passed he developed feelings for me and told me he was comfortable with me and never got that close to a person since he attempted suicide a few years earlier. He was on 23 different medications and I would give him natural remedies and pray for him daily. He told me that if I ever left him he didn't know what he would do. Immediately I felt sorry for him and knowing he attempted suicide made it even worse. I told him I had my place now and was moving out.

He literally cried and expressed to me that he didn't want to lose me. This man and I got married, and they Lord healed his body and he only had to take multivitamins. I took great care of this man as I would do anyone. The more I did, the more he did what he wanted to do. The spirit of depression was so strong on him to the point I was afraid to sleep next to him. I would always feel as though he would hurt me in my sleep.

He had a terrible habit of not paying bills or telling the truth. Instead, he would use bill money to shop at Dillard's. He lied about everything! We were in a situation where he didn't have a driver's license, so I had to drive everywhere. At the time I was the only one working and I was always on call working over 14 hours a day. It began to take a toll on my body. I prayed for him to get a job and he did. He realized that being with me benefited him which he stated to me.

One day this man was at work and his HR manager realized I was always dropping him off, so he gave him a car. I was super excited to see all these things happening. I would come home from work cook, clean and prepare the kids for school. All the while, he just sat at home on the computer, talked on the phone, or watched television day in and day out. He wouldn't speak to me and we weren't intimate.

I never cheated on him at all. However, I can't say the same about him. It got to the point where his phone would constantly ring and he would leave home and come back late. He said someone needed a ride. I never complained I accepted it.

Later on, I decided to get on Facebook. Upon logging on, I had received a message from a Ghanaian. We chatted, and it was like I became blinded all over again. Before I knew it, I got sucked right back into the trap of the enemy because my emotions were all over the place. I was already angry because I married a man that cheated and lied. Due to these bad habits of his, we lost our place as a result. One morning while sitting at home, I received a knock at the door, and it was a Sheriff. They said we have 24 hours to leave. All our bill money was in the closet with Dillard's clothing and expensive shoes - I mean thousands of dollars' worth of expensive shoes. Now here I am homeless again.

My children and I spent two weeks in a hotel as he walked out on us. I really wasn't even surprised. I just remembered praying for alignment and all kinds of hell broke loose.

After that, I went back to Ghana that February and while there I met with the Pastor I was chatting with on Facebook without realizing I was being set up. Both this pastor and another pastor were like brothers. By me being vulnerable, they were operating witchcraft on me. Here I am doing things I had no business doing. He told me because I benefited him that he needed my oil to operate. Because I refused, he said I had to return to the states.

Upon my return, I found out that he built an altar with the last of the money I sent him. He gathered other pastors and witches to come against me and tried to curse me spiritually and was speaking rejection over my life and finances so that nothing would work for me so that I would not prosper. At that moment of finding out what he had done, I literally felt sick in my body and I couldn't think.

When I came back to the country, the kids and I ended up staying a few months with my parents, Bishop and Mama. While there, I repented and got myself together. I had to grab every ounce of energy within me to pray and break this curse off myself. I knew the Word of God, and I knew prayer, so now it was time to put it into action.

Chapter 8

Since I was 12-years-Old, I had been getting prophetic words concerning ministry, marriage, business and wealth. All I kept saying was, "When will it happen?" I've heard it for so long I began to remember then let the rest go because it seemed impossible. The same church that I grew up in Pennsylvania was where people would always prophesy over my life and touch my hands, heart, eyes, and feet to cover me. They would give prophetic words about what the Lord would do in my life, but they never seem to be working. Now I see those things happening.

Although I knew The Word of God and that God is not a man that he should lie nor the son of man that he should repent, at times I would still doubt. I also knew that I needed accountability because of the oil that I carried. I used to attend many ministries but often I would intimidate the leaders because I was firm and wouldn't compromise. I always had respect but if the doctrine wasn't biblical, I refused to take part. That alone would cause many to speak negative towards me. I was at the point of no return! I had to follow the Lord because my life and my children's lives depended on it. God has been so faithful even when I was undeserving of it and continued to keep me when I should have fallen.

During this time my prayer life and revelation increased and intensified. The prophetic and healing anointing grew to the point where it almost scared me. I knew now was the time to go forth in what the Lord has destined me to be. I was no longer concerned about the naysayers because the task ahead of me was great! I had to press with everything in me. I was experiencing the power of God in ways that surprised me. I would pray and people instantly got healed. Many were healed and set free because of my obedience. I heard God in such a powerful way and people would confirm those were things only God knew. When I spoke, it would bring conviction and destinies would be altered forever.

While in intense prayer and fasting, three months later, I got a call that the Section 8 housing that I applied for a few years earlier came through. The children and I moved in and I felt stability. As time passed the Lord removed close friends and those like sisters to me. I was slandered, gossiped about and even rejected. I was the talk of the church! The sad part is these were the same people who would ask me for help, prayer, or financial help. I was angry because a few of them even saw me at my weakest point and many used that against me.

They said, "How can she pray like that and preach? Just look at her life - who does she think she is?" I've heard it all! Some got close enough just to find out things to spread to others. I had many monitors watching me.

Chapter 9

A few months later, I was asked to attend a church program to minister and while there I was standing next to a part of my destiny and didn't realize it. That same Saturday evening we all went out to eat as a group and that's when I noticed Charles Jr. That evening he was just watching me trying to get my attention, however, I ignored him. I was just trying to make sure I was as cautious as possible. I knew that in the past I made horrible choices and mistakes that I didn't want to experience again.

Sunday evening while at my then friend's mother's house, my friend said, "Why don't you call Charles and his brother?" I said okay let me do so! When Charles answered the phone, I was so nervous. That evening while we were hanging out downtown we spoke. I went inside a restaurant to grab a drink, and the woman was so fascinated with my accent that she gave me a lot of chicken. I then offered Charles some chicken and the others. As we walked away, I heard many of them saying "look at them." That evening we spoke about so much! I remember it like yesterday. He was such a breath of fresh air, something I wasn't used to.

As time passed, we hung out and I would attend church with him. I thought that if we were dating and maybe married one day, I'd like to know the teaching he's receiving. So I would attend his church and spend time with him. The kids loved him and him, as his son loved me. One afternoon my then two friends came by and we studied, and while studying someone said something that caught my attention. "Charles is too young for you and besides he isn't on the same spiritual level as you." At that point I knew he was a part of my destiny. Everyone tried their best to keep us away from each other even his ex-wife and mother. The same person who was supposed to protect him was siding with the person against him. His ex-wife did background checks on me.

A few months later Charles made up in his mind that no one would stop what God was doing in his life! He told me that the Lord said he was to marry me in order for me to receive the power I've been praying for. Only God knew what was in my heart and prayed about. Charles proposed to me on Good Friday and someone married us on April 3rd. Everything that I prayed for in a spouse God gave me! I wanted to live a pure and Holy Life before the Lord and with my obedience he granted it.

Chapter 10

"Now it is God who makes both us and you stand firm in Christ. He anointed us, sent his seal of ownership on us, and put his Spirit in our hearts as a deposit, guaranteeing what is to come." 2 Corinthians 1:21-22

Regardless of the setbacks we may have in our lives and from the past, God is faithful and never slack concerning his promises. Although we may choose another direction and alter our destiny, God knows the result!

The key is repentance and obedience! I had to realize that I wasn't perfect regardless of me knowing how to pray and quoting the Word. I had to acknowledge that I needed help and I couldn't do it on my own. My mind needed renewing. I realized that I couldn't afford to go through that hell again, and I had to totally surrender to God. Depression, anxiety and panic attacks no longer hospitalize me every two weeks. Mind battles had such a tight grip on me to the point I could barely function. All the doctors would do is give me prescriptions but I refused to accept them. I felt the moment I took those medicines, I would lose my mind for good! I needed deliverance, but no one had what it took to help me.

Right now, I am happier than I've ever been, and my children are doing well. My son struggled for years to tell me he loved me just because his father and grandmother had a demonic stronghold on him since he was six months old. Whenever he would hear their voices it would activate something. This year 2018, my son was set free! In the middle of deliverance service he vomited up a green slime substance that appeared to be glue like and told me that he feels better than ever. He now tells me he loves me daily and even hugs me!

I thank God that all is working in our favor. People's lives depend on our obedience, and I thank God we are aligned and awaiting the continued blessings of the Lord. I encourage you all to remain aligned and don't lose focus! Greater is already here and all you have to do is trust the process.

I know that many of you may find yourself somewhere within this book. Self-control played a big role also. I had to make up in my mind that I wanted change and I worked towards it. It wasn't easy by a longshot. I had to refrain from a lot of things, people, conversations and places. Self-control is having the ability to control one's emotions and desires or the expression of them in difficult situations. We must have self-discipline, restraint, composure and coolness.

There were many times I found myself wanting to go back to what was familiar because it was a comfortable place to me. I thank God for deliverance! Although I knew according to John 8:36 AMP "So if the Son makes you free, then you are unquestionably free." I was aware of that scripture but I realized I was in need of deliverance. Deliverance is something we constantly have to maintain. I had to stay away from certain things or music that I knew would make we feel a certain way. It was not easy! I had to read the Word of God daily, listen to more worship music, increase my prayer life and withhold from many conversations and phone calls. If I knew than an ex and I were not together, I wouldn't make or receive phone calls from them and I would ignore their calls.

Also, I tried to refrain from uncompromising situations as much as possible. Anything that took my focus or would make me dwell on my past, I quickly disengaged from. Whenever I began to feel anxious I would read Philippians 4:6-9 daily. "Do not be anxious or worried about anything, but in everything [every circumstance and situation] by prayer and petition with thanksgiving, continue to make your [specific] requests known to God. 7 And the peace of God [that peace which reassures the heart, that peace] which transcends all understanding, [that peace which] stands guard over your hearts and your minds in Christ Jesus [is yours].

8 Finally, believers, whatever is true, whatever is honorable and worthy of respect, whatever is right and confirmed by God's word, whatever is pure and wholesome, whatever is lovely and brings peace, whatever is admirable and of good repute; if there is any excellence, if there is anything worthy of praise, think continually on these things [center your mind on them, and implant them in your heart]. 9 The things which you have learned and received and heard and seen in me, practice these things [in daily life], and the God [who is the source] of peace and well-being will be with you."

Once I began to meditate on this word daily, it started becoming alive to me. I could literally feel my mind and thoughts shifting. The more I began to consecrate and pray, the more I started noticing a change within myself. My mind was clear and I was able to make sound decisions. At this point, I knew this change was permanent and I couldn't afford to go backward.

Everything about me changed! I began eating healthy again, smiling more, interacting with people I knew didn't like me and most of all I having so much joy. It was like I literally became a new person. Regardless of the stress of life, I was actually happy for the first time in my life. Now I can say that I truly love myself because for so long I tried to be something I wasn't. I thank God for the grace that he has given me to continue to persevere.

One thing I suggest is to pray for the renewing of your mind, surround yourself with Christ minded people who are able to pour into you, pray for TRUE discernment so that you are not lead astray or fooled and DO NOT disregard red flags.

I believe that since I was able to overcome my past, YOU can as well. You're not alone and God has you right where he wants you at this turning point.

Made in the USA
Columbia, SC
18 July 2021